Hello, Crabby!

Jonathan
Fenske

ACORN™
SCHOLASTIC INC.

For Pendy, who still laughs at my dad jokes.

All rights reserved. Published by Scholastic Inc., *Publishers since 1920*.
SCHOLASTIC, ACORN, and associated logos are trademarks
and/or registered trademarks of Scholastic Inc.

The publisher does not have any control over and does not assume any
responsibility for author or third-party websites or their content.

Library of Congress Cataloging-in-Publication Data

Names: Fenske, Jonathan, author.
Title: Hello, Crabby! / by Jonathan Fenske.
Description: First edition. | New York, NY : Acorn/Scholastic Inc., 2019. |
Series: Crabby | Summary: Crabby is not a happy crab, in fact Crabby is quite crabby,
so pushy Plankton, who is always trying to cheer up fellow marine creatures,
bakes Crabby a cake—but will Crabby finally smile?
Identifiers: LCCN 2018033264| ISBN 9781338281507 (pbk) | ISBN 9781338281514 (hardcover)
Subjects: LCSH: Crabs—Juvenile fiction. | Plankton—Juvenile fiction. |
Cake—Juvenile fiction. | Cheerfulness—Juvenile fiction. | CYAC:
Crabs—Fiction. | Plankton—Fiction. | Cake—Fiction. |
Cheerfulness—Fiction. | Humorous stories. | LCGFT: Humorous fiction. |
Picture books. Classification: LCC PZ7.F34843 He 2019 | DDC (E)—dc23 LC record available
at https://lccn.loc.gov/2018033264

10 9 8 7 6 5 4 3   19 20 21 22 23

Printed in China   62

First edition, May 2019

Edited by Katie Carella
Book design by Marissa Asuncion

The **sun** in my eyes.

The **salt** in my teeth.

The **sand** in my shell.

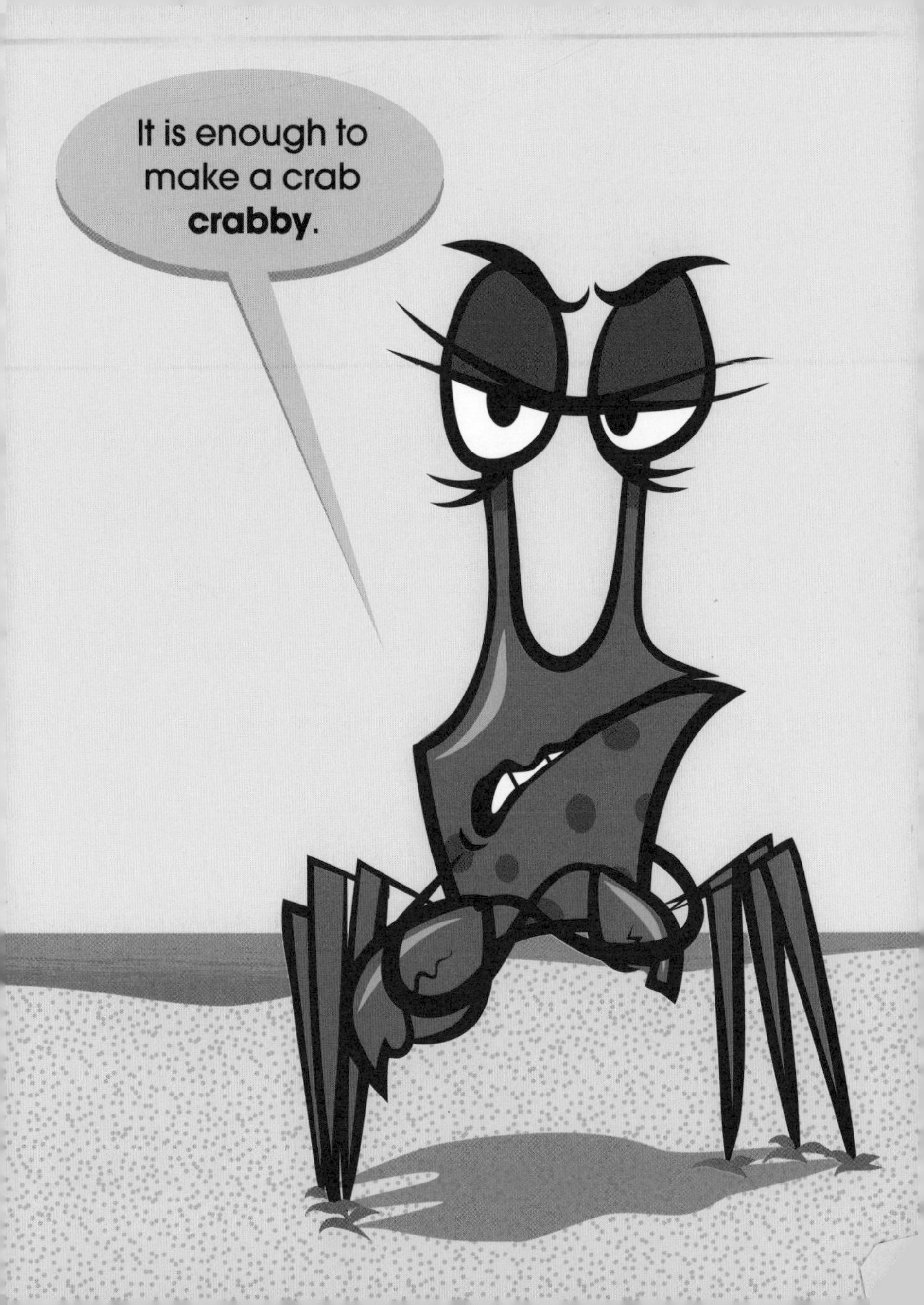
It is enough to make a crab **crabby**.

I can dig
a hole.

I can watch
the ocean
fill it up.

I can dig
a hole
again.

I can scuttle to the dunes.

I can scuttle to the water.

I can sit **right here**.

Wow.

So many choices.

Well, it looks like today is a **SCUTTLE-TO-THE-WATER** day.

THINGS TO DO:
scuttle to the water

7

THE CRABBY CRAB

Oh, great. Here comes that **pushy** Plankton.

Good morning, Crabby!

Hmmmph.

I said, **good morning, Crabby!**

What is so **good** about it?

15

Look at the **blue** skies!

I prefer **gray**.

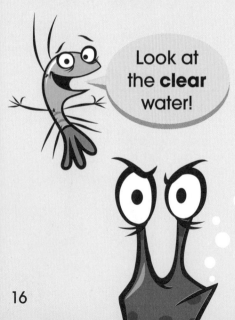

Look at the **clear** water!

I prefer **cloudy**.

16

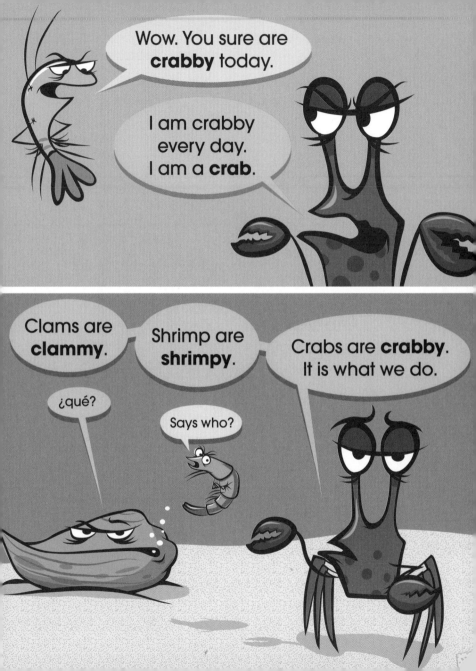

Well, Abby is a crab. And **she** is not crabby.

La, la, la!

Tabby is a crab. And **she** is not crabby.

La, la, la!

Blabby is a crab. And **he** is not crabby.

La, la, la!

Blah, blah, blah!

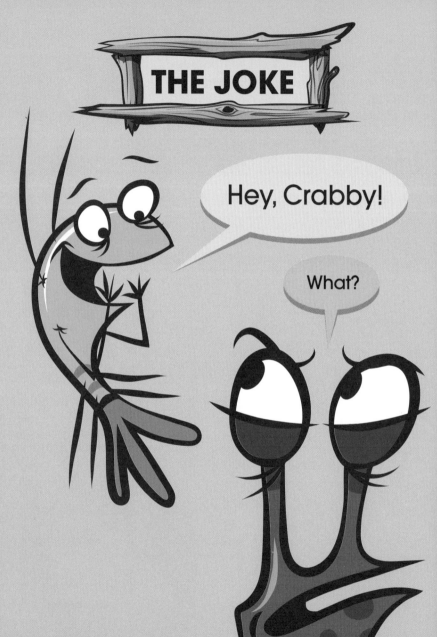

21

So, you would probably **not** be crabby if I told you a really funny joke?

No. It is probably **not** a really funny joke.

I **promise** it will tickle your funny bone!

Crabs do not **have** bones.

SMACK!

Well?
Do you want to
hear the joke?

Not really.

I will take
that as
a **yes**.

Why did
the crab
cross the
ocean?

23

24

That was the joke?

I told you it wasn't funny.

AAARGH!

Let me show you how this works.

THE CAKE

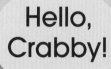

Hello, Crabby!

If I told you I baked you an **awesome** cake, would you still be crabby?

31

33

But your **crabby** is making me **CRAZY!**

And your **crazy** is making me **MORE CRABBY!**

Well.

You won't be crabby when you see this cake.

Yes, I will probably **still** be crabby.

Ooh. Did I just see a little **smile**?

No.

I am pretty sure that was a smile.

It was **not** a smile.

Uh-huh. Well, a yummy chocolate cake would make **me** smile.

It was NOT a smile!

And for the record, I prefer **lemon** cake.

GASP!

GASP! GASP!

So, are you going to eat some cake?

I was not planning on it.

TAP TAP

TWITCH TWITCH

Oh, all right.
Give me some cake.

Well?

WELL?

WELL?!

It is a little **dry**.

AAARGH!

Crabby is **TOO CRABBY**!

About the Author

Jonathan Fenske lives in South Carolina with his family. He was born in Florida near the ocean, so he knows all about life at the beach! Sea creatures never baked him a cake, but he would have **loved** Plankton's cake because chocolate is his favorite flavor.

Jonathan is the author and illustrator of several children's books including **Barnacle Is Bored**, **Plankton Is Pushy** (a Junior Library Guild selection), and the LEGO® picture book **I'm Fun, Too!** His early reader **A Pig, a Fox, and a Box** was a Theodor Seuss Geisel Honor Book.

YOU CAN DRAW CRABBY!

YIPPEE.

1. Draw two ovals and connect them with a "U" to make eyes.

2. Draw the body.

3. Add six legs and one mouth.

4. Draw two arms and two claws. (One claw should be bigger.)

5. Add the details.

6. Color in your drawing!

WHAT'S YOUR STORY?

Plankton bakes Crabby a cake.
What kind of cake would **you** bake for Crabby?
What would your cake look like?
Would your cake make Crabby smile?
Write and draw your story!

scholastic.com/acorn